Beth Stewart

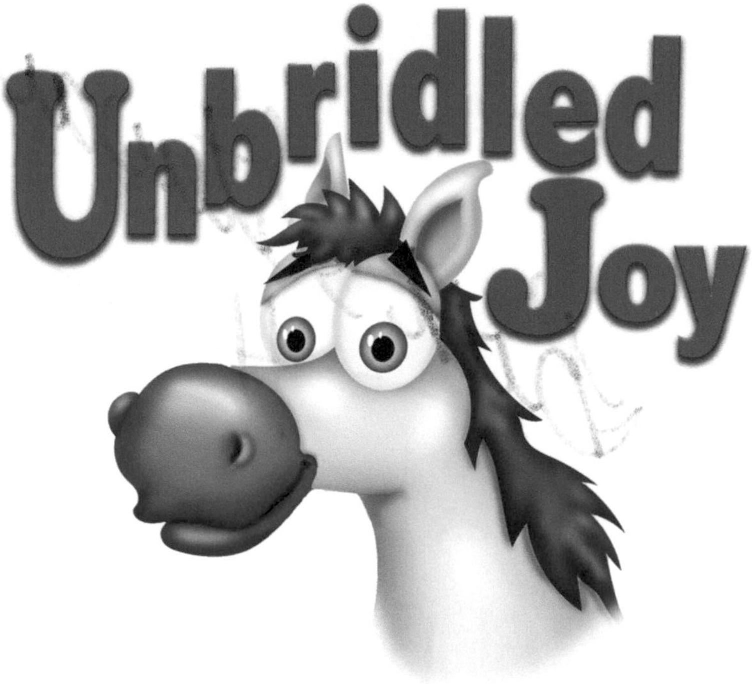
Unbridled Joy

Dedication to my two sons, Alex and Austin,
for helping to foster my love for reading to children.

Joy bucked when he saw his owner with a bridle in his hand. "A saddle is bad enough, but I hate that thing," squealed Joy.

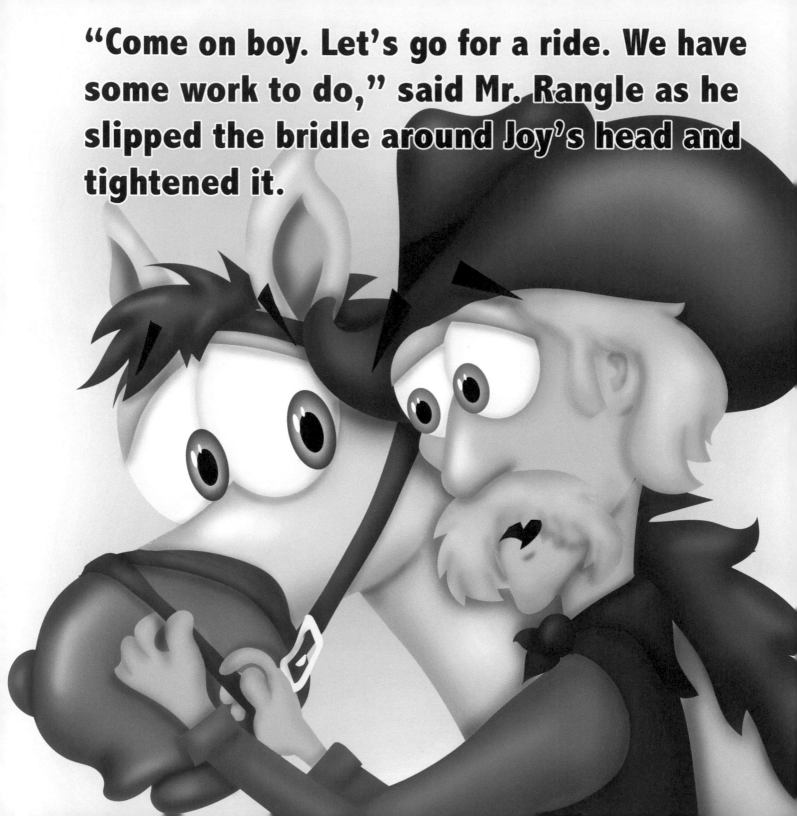

"Come on boy. Let's go for a ride. We have some work to do," said Mr. Rangle as he slipped the bridle around Joy's head and tightened it.

The horse swayed his head, but his owner didn't pay any attention. Mr. Rangle eased his foot into the stirrup, slid up onto Joy, and off they went.

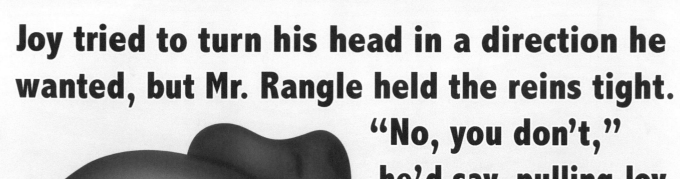

Joy tried to turn his head in a direction he wanted, but Mr. Rangle held the reins tight. "No, you don't," he'd say, pulling Joy in the direction he needed to go.

Riding the range, Joy spotted a wild mustang running free. The mustang went in any direction he wanted. *That's what I want*, **he thought.** *I want to be free like the mustang. I don't want to be bridled.*

After their ride, Mr. Rangle brought Joy back in the stable. He took off Joy's bridle and saddle. He brushed him down and gave him a piece of apple. Then he put Joy in his stall. "See you later, boy."

Joy whinnied and kicked the door. "What's the matter?" asked Roscoe from the next stall.

"I'm tired of being bridled," said Joy. "I'm tired of being led around, having to do whatever Mr. Rangle wants. This is no life. I want to be free."

"Not me," said Roscoe. "We have food, we're taken care of, and we have friends here. It's a good life."

Joy shook his head. "I see the wild mustang when I'm on the range. He's his own master. He's free to do what he wants, when he wants. And, he doesn't have to wear a bridle to be led around."

From that moment, Joy made up his mind to escape.

The next day when he and the other horses were put in the paddock to graze, he eyed the fence. "I can do this," he whispered.

Joy backed up, then raced toward the fence. Soaring over it, freedom surged through him.

When he landed, he galloped as fast and as far as he could.

After a long while, Joy stopped. Catching his breath, he noticed that nothing looked familar. "I did it!" he cried. "I'm free! I'm my own master! No more bridles or bits for me." With his newfound freedom, Joy wandered where ever he wanted.

When the sun set and a blanket of darkness covered the land, Joy heard the howls of hungry coyotes.

Snorting, he galloped off. He didn't know where he was going. He was too scared to care.

Joy galloped until he couldn't gallop any longer. With his chest heaving, he began to cry. "Where can I go to be safe?"

Just then Joy heard a loud whinny. "Who's there?" Joy backed up until he was up against a tree.

Another loud whinny came. Then the horse came into focus...

... It was the wild mustang!
"What are you doing in my territory?"
asked the mustang. "You
don't belong here."

Joy moved a little closer. "Y-You're the
mustang. I've watched you run free. I
ran away to be free like you."

The mustang reared up then stomped his feet as he eyed Joy. "The wild life is not for everyone. Can you outrace coyotes?"

"Can you fight them off if you need to? Can you stay alone, with no friends or family?"

"Uh, I don't think so," muttered Joy.

"Well," said the mustang, "can you protect yourself from other dangerous animals in the wilderness? Can you live on only grass and leaves?"

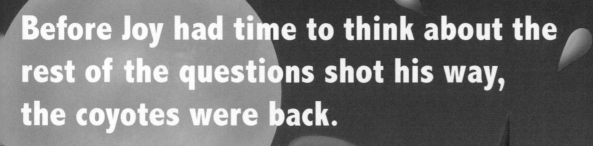

Before Joy had time to think about the rest of the questions shot his way, the coyotes were back.

In a blur, the mustang was gone. Hungry growls came from all directions. They got closer and closer.

Suddenly, Joy saw them as the moonlight shone through the branches of the trees.

Joy squealed and reared
up. He kicked
his front legs.

As soon as the coyotes
backed away, Joy jumped
over them and
ran for his life.

Without thinking, Joy raced in the direction he had come. Even when his legs felt like collapsing, he raced on.

Joy wiggled his head and actually smiled at his owner. He was finally happy.